Con

Series Reading Consultant: Prue Goodwin
National Centre for Language and Literacy,
University of Reading

The Were-Pig

Paul Stewart

Illustrated by Tony Ross

www.kidsatrandomhouse.co.uk

For Anna

*Also available by Paul Stewart,
and published by Corgi Pups Books:*

DOGBIRD

THE WERE-PIG
A CORGI PUPS BOOK: 0 552 547131

First publication in Great Britain

PRINTING HISTORY
Corgi Pups edition published 2002

3 5 7 9 10 8 6 4

Set in 18/25pt Bembo MT Schoolbook

Corgi Books are published by Random House Children's Books,
61–63 Uxbridge Road, London W5 5SA,
a division of The Random House Group Ltd,
in Australia by Random House Australia (Pty) Ltd,
20 Alfred Street, Milsons Point, Sydney, NSW 2061, Australia,
in New Zealand by Random House New Zealand Ltd,
18 Poland Road, Glenfield, Auckland 10, New Zealand
and in South Africa by Random House (Pty) Ltd,
Endulini, 5a Jubilee Road, Parktown 2193, South Africa

Made and printed in Great Britain
by Cox & Wyman Ltd, Reading, Berkshire

Chapter One

"You did *what*?" exclaimed Nan Tucker.

"I took a Mars bar from Joanne's lunch-box," said Albert.

"And did you eat it?"

Albert blushed and looked down at the floor.

"Well?" she said.

Albert nodded. "Yes," he admitted.

Nan Tucker breathed in noisily. "But this is serious," she said. "Very serious."

Albert Amis was nine. Two years earlier his parents had split up, and his dad left home for good.

Mum had tried to cope on her own, but it wasn't easy. She had to leave for work at seven in the morning, and never got home before seven in the evening.

When the summer holidays came around, the situation became impossible. That was when Nan Tucker moved in with them.

Nan Tucker was Albert's mum's mum. Tall and skinny, with bright red hair and dark green eyes, she wasn't like any other grandmothers that Albert knew. None of *them* wore long patchwork skirts or had beads plaited into their hair.

But Albert wouldn't have had Nan Tucker any other way. She was fun. She played the guitar, and told brilliant stories. She took him on long walks – and never minded him keeping the things his mum would have made him

leave behind, like owl-pellets and
beetles and the skeletons of
small animals and birds. She
showed him how to make
things, too – a robot, a radio
and chocolate chip cookies.

And when Albert had
wanted a pet, it
was Nan Tucker
who persuaded
his mum to let
him have the
white rat he'd
set his heart
on.

All in all,
Nan Tucker was the perfect
grandmother – which was why
her reaction to the Mars bar
was so worrying. If Nan Tucker
said it was serious, then Albert
knew it really was serious.

"But it's not fair!" he said. "Joanne had a Mars bar, a Kit-Kat *and* a bag of wine gums. All I had was one of those boring muesli chews – and I hate them."

"Then you should have told me," said Nan Tucker. "Anything, rather than letting your greed get the better of you."

Albert winced. He could still see the Mars bar nestled up in the corner of Joanne's lunch-box, and Joanne herself, busy talking to Ella. He'd slipped his

hand inside the lunch-box,
shoved the chocolate bar up his
sleeve and left before Joanne
noticed it was missing. Then,
outside on the school field, he'd
pulled off the wrapper and
eaten it all in one go. It had
tasted delicious.

"One last question," said Nan Tucker. "Was the sun shining?"

Albert thought back. "Yes," he said.

"Oh, dear," said Nan Tucker. "Oh, dearie-dear! Such a display of greed, and by the light of the full-sun! Do you know what this means, Albert?"

Albert shook his head.
"What?" he said.

"Unless I'm very much mistaken – and I seldom am," she added, "you have brought upon yourself the curse of the were-pig!"

Chapter Two

"Were-pig?" said Albert
alarmed. "I've heard of a were-*wolf*, but . . ."

"Were-wolf? *Pah!*" said Nan
Tucker. "There's no such thing.

All that howling at the full-
moon nonsense! A were-*pig*, on
the other hand, is all too real."

"But what is it?" asked Albert.

"A greedy monster," came the hushed reply. "Half-human, half pig. It emerges when the sun is full . . ."

"This is just one of your stories, right?" said Albert, laughing uneasily. "I mean,  for a start, the sun is always full."

"Precisely," said Nan Tucker darkly.

"I . . . I don't understand," said Albert.

"Greed drove you to take that Mars bar in broad daylight," said Nan Tucker. "Now, whenever the sun appears from behind the clouds, that same greed will change you into a were-pig. Snout, trotters, curly tail – the whole caboodle."

"No," Albert gasped. "It can't be true."

"Oh, but it can," said Nan Tucker. "If it wasn't dark outside now, you'd see."

"But how long will it last?" said Albert. "A day? A month? For ever?"

Nan Tucker shrugged. "That, I cannot say."

Albert found it hard to go to sleep
that night. Of course, he knew
Nan Tucker was only joking –

she'd just been trying to frighten him so that he'd never take anything from anyone again. There was no such thing as a were-pig. How could there be?

And yet . . .

What if there was? What if he really did turn into a were-pig? What *then*?

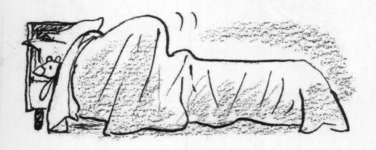

The next morning, Albert woke
early. He jumped out of bed,
ran to the window and peeked
out through the curtains.

Heavy rain was falling from a
dark, cloudy sky.

"Thank goodness for that!"
he said.

After breakfast, Albert put on his shoes and waterproof. Nan Tucker handed him his lunch-box at the door.

"I put a Mars bar in," she said, and winked. "Have a lovely day, Albert."

"I will," said Albert. He was
pleased she hadn't mentioned
the business of the were-pig. It
must have been a joke.

Joke or no joke, Albert couldn't stop thinking about the curse of the were-pig. All through numeracy-hour he kept checking to see that it hadn't stopped raining.

"Albert!" Mrs Wilkinson
snapped at last. "If I catch you
looking out of the window once
more, I'll keep you in at break."

"Sorry, Mrs Wilkinson," said
Albert. "It won't happen again."

But it did.

At a quarter to ten, the rain had turned to light drizzle. At ten o'clock it had stopped completely. And at a quarter past, Albert was dismayed to see  the sun glowing brightly behind the thinning clouds. Uh-oh, he thought.

"That's it, Albert!" Mrs Wilkinson shouted. "You will not go out to play." Ten minutes later, the bell went. While all the other children streamed out of the class and into the playground, followed by Mrs Wilkinson, Albert stayed in his seat.

And there he remained, tired
after his broken night's sleep,
while outside, the hidden sun
grew warmer and brighter.

He laid his head on his elbow
and stared miserably out of
the window through half-closed
eyes. Any moment now, the sun
would burst through the clouds.
Any moment . . .

Chapter Three

"Aargh!" Albert shrieked, as dazzling beams of sunlight streamed down from the sky. 'Aaar . . . *weeeiiiii!*"

Albert fell still, horrified by

the noise he had just made. It
had definitely been a squeal. His
hand shot up to his mouth.

"Oink!" he grunted in horror
as his fingers touched, not his
mouth, but a snout.

"Oink!" he grunted again as his hands twisted and hardened, to form two trotters.

He reached round anxiously – and there it was: a short, curly tail sticking out from a hole in his trouser. "OI-INK!"

It had happened! Albert had changed into a were-pig.

What was worse, the terrible transformation had left him feeling hungrier than he'd ever felt before. He had to eat something; anything – *everything!* Now!

As he headed for the door, Albert found that walking on two legs was too

difficult with all the extra
weight he had to carry. With a
sigh, he dropped down onto all
fours. Along the corridor he
scurried, round a corner, past
reception and into the
dining-hall – drawn on by
the snout-watering smells
wafting from the kitchen.

The dinner-ladies were setting up the tables and chairs. They didn't see Albert darting across the floor.

So far, so good, he thought as, head down, he charged at the swing doors. With a thud, they burst open. Albert ran inside and squealed with delight.

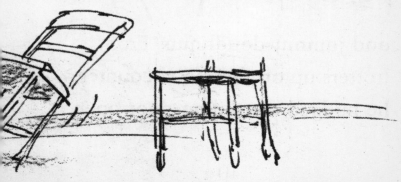

Food! He was surrounded
by food!

First off, Albert made for
the warming-cabinet. Inside it
were pies and pasties, hot-dogs
and burgers, apple turnovers

and jammy-doughnuts. Front
trotters up on the metal counter,
he nudged the sliding-door open

with his snout, thrust his head inside and began gorging himself.

Sweet or savoury, it didn't matter. The air was soon filled with splattered jam and gravy, and a flurry of flaky pastry.

Within minutes every last morsel
was gone — and Albert was
hungrier than ever.

He heaved himself up onto the
serving-counter and waddled
along the row of steel containers.
Each one held something more
delicious than the last.

Hotpot . . .
Baked beans . . .
Chips . . .
Chocolate
pudding . . .
Caramel sauce . . .
Albert plunged his head into
every single one of them, and
guzzled down the food in great,
greedy mouthfuls.

And *still* he was hungry!
Looking round, Albert's
attention was
caught by a
huge steam-
ing pot on
the stove. He
sniffed — once,

twice — and a
smile spread
over his
piggy
features. It
was his
favourite.
Custard.

Albert took a flying leap
through the air – forgetting
for a moment that pigs *can't* fly

– and careered into the great
pot of custard. The pot toppled
backwards and fell to the floor
with a loud *crash*! The custard
went everywhere.

But Albert didn't care. He dropped down after it, pushed his snout into the sweet, yellow goo, and began slurping noisily.

Unfortunately, the dinner-
ladies had also heard the crash.

"What was that?"
shouted one.

"I'll check!"
shouted another.

Grunting with
frustration, Albert abandoned the
delicious custard. He trotted off
and hid himself under the sink.

"What on earth . . !" he
heard the dinner-lady exclaim.
"Madge! Vera! Come and look
at this!"

Albert kept as quiet as he
could. He didn't want to be
spotted – and if it hadn't been
for the slop-bucket,
he might not
have been. But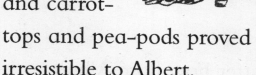
the delicious
smell of the
potato-peel
and carrot-
tops and pea-pods proved
irresistible to Albert.

He leaned forwards. He
pushed his head deep down
into the bucket – and got it
stuck fast.

Chapter Four

No matter how hard Albert
shook his head, or tried to prise
the bucket off with his trotters,
he could not free himself. The
bucket would not budge. What

was worse, the shrieking of the
dinner-ladies was coming closer.

"I've got to get
out of here," Albert
snorted. "And quick!"
He jumped up
and dashed across the
kitchen. With the bucket over his
head, he couldn't see a thing.

He blundered
around
noisily,
desperately
trying to
find a way
out.

"It's a pig!" the dinner-ladies were screaming. "And it's been at the food!"

Albert felt two rough hands grasp his curly tail.

Squealing with indignation, he pulled away, skidded off over the slippery floor and . . .

THUD!

For a moment, Albert thought he'd hit the wall. But no. At last, he'd had some good luck. He'd found the swing-doors and was back inside the dining-hall.

As he tried to cross the floor,
Albert soon discovered that the
dining-hall was an even worse
place to be than the kitchen.
Whichever way he turned he
knocked into things.

Bang! Clatter! CRASH!
Leaving behind him a tangled
mass of tables and chairs, Albert
ran blindly down a corridor.

Then another. And another. He
didn't know where he was now.
Everywhere seemed the same.

Finally, Albert gave up. He sat
down heavily on
the floor and
closed his eyes.
He had no
choice but to
wait for some-
one to come
and help him.

"Oink," he grunted sadly.
Now everyone would discover
his terrible secret. "Oink!"

"Albert Amis!" came an angry
voice. "Is
that you?"

Albert froze. It was Mrs
Wilkinson. He felt two hands
seize the bucket and pull it off
his head.

"What on earth are you
doing sitting on the floor with
the waste-paper bin on your
head?" she said.

"I . . . I . . ." Albert stammered. He reached up nervously and touched . . . his mouth. And with fingers, not trotters. He felt round for the curly tail, but that too had gone.

"Clowning about," said Mrs Wilkinson, answering her own question. "And I'll have no more of it. Do you understand?"

"Yes, Mrs Wilkinson. Sorry, Mrs Wilkinson," he said.

He was a boy again, not a were-pig – even with the full-sun streaming in through the windows of his classroom.

The bell rang, and the rest of
the class began filing back to their
tables.

"And from now on," said
Albert, "I promise I'll be good."
And this time, he was.

★

"How was school today?" Nan Tucker called when she heard the front-door closing.

"Fine," said Albert. He'd decided to keep quiet about the were-pig incident. She'd only worry. "Except for one thing."

Nan Tucker
appeared from the
kitchen, drying
her hands on
a tea-towel.
"What was
that?" she
said.

"The Mars
bar you said you put in my
lunch-box," said
Albert. "When
I went to
eat it, it
wasn't
there."

"Wasn't there?" said Nan Tucker, her eyes gleaming mischievously. "Do you think someone could have taken it?"

Albert shook his head. "Perhaps," he said.

"Well, more fool them if they have," said Nan Tucker. "They'll have brought the curse of the were-pig down on themselves.

And if the curse is on *them* then it's no longer on *you*!" She frowned. "But be careful, Albert. Next time you might not be so lucky."

"Next time?" said Albert. "There's not going to be a next time. Ever."

Nan Tucker smiled. "Good," she said. "That's *just* what I wanted to hear!'

THE END